A Dream Come True

Coming to America from Vietnam —1975

M. J. Cosson

Perfection Learning®

Cover Design: Tobi Cunningham
Inside Illustration: Winson Trang was born in Vietnam
to Chinese parents. He currently resides in
southern California. He is represented by Creative
Freelancers.

Cover Image Credit: Corbis

Acknowledgment

Many thanks to Carmen Richardson, Richard
G. Freeman, and Dr. Thuy Danh Do for your
thoughtful reviews of this story.

Paperback ISBN 0-7891-5509-5
Cover Craft® ISBN 0-7569-0290-8

Table *of* Contents

Introduction

❧

Vietnam in 1975

In 1975, after nearly 100 years, warfare in Vietnam was ending. Beginning in 1858, Vietnam had been a French colony. Along with Cambodia and Laos, it was known as Indochina. Over and over, the Vietnamese people **rebelled** against the French. But the rebellions were not successful.

In the early 1940s, World War II was raging. Vietnam was caught in the middle. Japan was fighting for one side. France was fighting for the other. Both wanted to control Vietnam.

A **Communist** named Ho Chi Minh formed a group of fighters. They were called the **Vietminh**.

The Vietminh was a **front** for Ho Chi Minh's real desires. These fighters wanted independence for

Vietnam. Ho Chi Minh wanted to lead the independent country under Communism.

During WWII, the Vietminh fought Japan. Toward the end of the war, Ho Chi Minh declared Vietnam a free nation. He declared himself the leader. He used words from the United States Constitution. He wanted America to back Vietnam. But the U.S. did not help Vietnam in its fight against the French.

Once again, France occupied Vietnam. A war between France and the Vietminh began. The Vietminh knew **guerrilla warfare**. They were terrorists. They set off bombs in public places to kill and frighten people. The Vietminh won the war with France.

Vietnam split into two separate countries. North Vietnam was Communist. South Vietnam was **democratic**. But Ho Chi Minh continued fighting with South Vietnam to bring it under the control of Communist North Vietnam.

Around the world, the Soviet Union and China were spreading Communism to other countries. The U.S. and other free countries feared the spread of Communism.

The U.S. offered aid to South Vietnam to keep Communism out. At first, the U.S. sent military people over to train South Vietnamese soldiers. But by the 1960s, U.S. soldiers were fighting the North Vietnamese too.

Other countries, such as Great Britain, also helped South Vietnam. The Soviet Union and China helped North Vietnam.

The fighting dragged on for many years. During that time, Ho Chi Minh died.

In 1973, a treaty was signed, and the U.S. was no longer involved in the war. By that time, 3.4 million Americans had served in Vietnam.

But the fighting between North and South Vietnam continued. In

April of 1975, South Vietnam lost the war. North and South Vietnam became one Communist country—Vietnam.

Many South Vietnamese left their homeland. The Communist government tortured and killed many of the South Vietnamese leaders who stayed behind. Others were sent to prisons for many years.

COMING *to* AMERICA
from VIETNAM
1975

AMERICA

VIETNAM

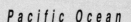

Pacific Ocean

1

1985—Michigan U.S.A.

The **bobber** dipped under the water. Cammy felt a small tug on the line. She gave the pole a quick jerk. She felt a bigger tug.

Cammy looked at the place where the bobber used to be. The line zipped through the water.

"I got one!" she cried.

"Hold on," her dad said. "This could be a big one."

They watched as the line zipped back and forth in the water.

"It *is* a big one!" Cammy cried. "Look how much it's bending the pole."

"Reel it in slowly," Dad said.

Cammy held on to the fishing pole with her right hand. With her left, she turned the reel. Slowly, the fishing line came closer to the boat. Her dad was ready with the fishnet.

"This thing must weigh 20 pounds," Cammy said. Her hand was shaking from the effort.

"Do you need help?" Dad asked.

Cammy looked at him. "For Pete's sake, Dad. I can do it. I am 12 years old," she said.

"But a big one can wear out the best fisher," her dad said. "There's nothing wrong with asking for help."

"I know," Cammy said. "But I'm okay. Really."

"You've got it hooked. Give the line

some play. Let it wear itself out."

"Last time I did that, I lost it," Cammy said.

Her dad shrugged. "It's your fish," he said.

Cammy wound the reel tighter. Now the line was next to the boat. Her dad dipped the net into the water. He brought up a huge catfish.

"Wow!" Cammy said when she saw what she had caught.

Her dad flipped the big fish out onto the bottom of the boat. The fish flopped around. Its face had whiskers like a cat.

"We can have a feast tonight," Dad said. He put the fish in the old cooler. "There's enough of that fish to feed the whole family. Grandma and Grandpa too."

Cammy looked proud. She baited her hook again. The worm wiggled as she threaded it on to the hook.

Cammy cast the line into the water. Then she washed the worm scum off her hands.

Cammy leaned back in the boat. Her long black ponytail hung over the side. The end dipped into the water. The warm sun felt good on her face.

The only sound was the gentle lapping of the waves against the boat. A bird called in the distance. It was a peaceful moment.

A good time for a story, Cammy thought. She looked at her dad.

"Dad, will you tell me the story?"

"What story?"

"You know the one."

2

1973—Pleiku, Vietnam

Cammy's dad began.

"I was 20 when I was **drafted** into the army. I was a soldier during the Vietnam War. I was sent to the center of Vietnam. In the mountains. Near a place called **Pleiku**.

"The war was like the U.S. Civil War in one way. The North fought the South. Sometimes people in the same family were on different sides.

"But in Vietnam, other countries helped both sides," he continued. "The battles weren't like the battles of the Civil War. Back then, it was clear who the enemy was. In Vietnam, it was sometimes hard to tell.

"My job was to look for the **Vietcong**. They were fighting for the North. The Communist side. But a Vietcong could be anybody.

"We checked villages. We had Vietnamese **interpreters**. We asked questions of the villagers. Our interpreters told us what the people said." Cammy's dad paused a moment.

"The men in my company had to go through each hut," he said. "We had to look in every hiding place. It was our job to keep the villagers safe. It was our job to kill or capture the Vietcong. And they were hard to find."

"Why was that?" Cammy asked. When

her dad got to this part, she always asked that question.

Cammy's dad looked at her. This time he didn't answer.

"Why do you think?" he asked.

"Because some were the brothers of the people in the huts. Because they didn't all wear uniforms. Because they had secret hiding places. And because they were very smart," Cammy answered.

"Yes. All of those reasons. And one other thing," her dad said.

"What's that?" Cammy asked.

"The Vietcong may have been hard to find because they weren't even there," he replied.

Cammy laughed.

"It sounds funny now. But it wasn't funny then," her dad said. "We never knew when we might get **ambushed**. We always had to be on guard. It wasn't just a walk through a village. It wasn't a game of hide-and-seek."

"What about the people?" Cammy asked. She always asked that question too.

"Your turn again," her dad said. "How do you think the people in the villages felt?"

"I think they were scared," Cammy said.

Her dad nodded. "I think they were scared too," he said.

Cammy looked at her dad.

"Now tell about that day. Please," she begged.

3

About That Day

Cammy's dad looked up at the sky. He took a deep breath. Cammy could tell that her dad was glad to be on this side of the world with her. He was glad to be safe in a fishing boat on a sunny day.

For a minute, Cammy thought her dad was going to say something like "Isn't it a nice day?" But he didn't. He took another deep breath. Then he began again.

"One day, we visited a village high in the mountains. We knew something was wrong right away.

"We walked down the road," he continued. "It was too quiet. I went into the first hut. No one was there.

"Then I heard a sound. Like a kitten mewing. I went to the next hut. The sound came from under a mat. A baby was there. A little girl.

"The baby was very tiny," he explained. "She lay under that mat. All by herself. Who knows how long she'd been there. She didn't cry. She just made the mewing sounds.

"We found some bodies in the other huts. They had been shot.

"We never knew what happened. Did the Vietcong attack the village? Did the people just run away?

"Some of us took the baby back to

the base. Others went to check nearby fields and forests.

"I held the baby girl on the way back," Cammy's dad said. "When we got to the base, I mixed some powdered milk and fed her. We didn't have a baby bottle. I fed her from a soda bottle.

"She was very hungry. She stared into my eyes as she drank the milk. Then she fell asleep. She woke up a couple more times and stared at me.

"The baby never smiled. Not even a little grin. And she never cried. She just stared. I'd never seen such a sad look. It's almost as if she knew something.

"I held that baby girl until the next day. Then a helicopter took her to an **orphanage** in **Saigon**. I hated to let her go. I felt like it was my job to protect her.

"That night, I wrote your mom about the baby. I said I didn't think I would ever be able to forget how she looked into my eyes."

4

Operation Babylift

Cammy's dad continued the story.
He had a faraway look in his eyes.

"A month later, I was sent home. My year in Vietnam was over. I served the rest of my time at an army base in Maryland. Your mother came to live with me.

"I guess I talked about that baby a lot," he said. "Finally, your mother said, 'Why don't we see if we can find her? Maybe we can adopt her.'

"So we set the plan in motion. We talked to people. We filled out forms. There was lots of paperwork. But we didn't give up.

"Then we waited," he said. "And then we waited some more.

"In 1973, U.S. troops had **pulled out** of Vietnam. It happened shortly after I left. Many American people had not wanted us to be there. They felt our young men and women were dying for a lost cause.

"Then in 1975, the North Vietnamese took over South Vietnam.

"At the last minute, the U.S. tried to get as many orphans as possible out of the country. The effort was called Operation Babylift.

"The first airplane took off on April 4, 1975," Cammy's dad said. "About 240 children and some adults were on the plane. Soon after takeoff, something went wrong. The plane crashed. We learned that our baby was on that plane.

"Seventy-eight children were killed," her dad said sadly. "It was a very sad time. But a small miracle happened. Most of the children lived.

"The people at Operation Babylift didn't have time to mourn. The North Vietnamese were on their way. Hundreds of children still needed to get out of the country. Another plane took off the next day. It held the children who had lived plus more.

"That plane made it to the United States." He looked at Cammy.

"At last, the plane landed," he continued. "We were at Travis Air Force Base in California. We were so excited to meet our new daughter.

"The big C5-A touched down. Nurses and other people came out.

Each one held two or three children. We stared as each one walked by.

"At last, we saw our girl." Cammy's dad grinned. "Finally, I got to hold her again. I got to look into those beautiful brown eyes. Two years had passed. You had grown. But I knew it was you.

"I never knew your Vietnamese name. In the orphanage, they had called you Cam. So we named you Cammy."

5

Back to 1985

Cammy smiled at her dad. "And this is where I say, 'I'm glad you did.' "

Cammy grew quiet. Her gaze shifted to the water. "Is there anything more about me? Anything you haven't told me before?"

"No," her dad said. "You know everything I know."

"Sometimes I wonder if I have anybody left over there," Cammy said. "I wonder if my family ran away that day. And when they went back, I was gone. They didn't know where to find me. Do you think that could have happened?"

"Could be," her dad answered.

"You know, I'm pretty big now," Cammy said. "If you saw that my family was dead, you could tell me. I could take it."

"I know," Dad said. "But, Cammy, I didn't see anybody. I've told you that we went back a few days later. Nothing had changed. No one was there."

Cammy's dad gave her a hug. "I'm afraid you're stuck with us for a family."

Cammy hugged her dad back. Then she stared into her dad's eyes like she had 12 years before.

"You know I love you and Mom," she said. "You're my parents. Jill, Janelle, and Jamie are my sisters. But sometimes, I wonder about things."

Her dad shrugged. "Of course you do. I do too."

He started the motor.

"It's about time to get this fish home. We have to clean and gut it for supper."

"But the best part comes first," Cammy said. "First I get to show it to everybody. I can't wait for Grandpa to see it."

Grandpa took a picture of Cammy holding the big catfish. Then together they cleaned it. Grandma cooked Cammy's prize fish. She served it on a platter. It had lettuce and lemon and orange slices all around it. It looked beautiful.

For supper, they ate catfish, brown rice, green beans, and fruit salad.

"This is almost like a Vietnamese meal," Dad said.

"Yeah, rice and fish," Cammy said.

"The Vietnamese eat lots of fruit too," Mom said.

"It's time you learned more about your homeland, Cammy. I think we should start with Vietnamese food," she added. "And maybe some of the customs."

Cammy looked at her mom. Amazing, Cammy thought. It's almost scary. How did she know what I was thinking?

6

Sweet Rice and Chopsticks

"We'll start with sweet rice," Mom said the next day. "It's something I've fixed before. And I remember you liked it a lot."

"Why did we quit eating it then?" Cammy asked.

"I guess we forgot about it," her mom said. "When you were little, we tried some Vietnamese foods. But then your sisters came along. And we forgot that you are Vietnamese."

"You didn't really forget," Cammy said.

"Yes," her mom said. "I really did. You were just Cammy. We didn't mean to forget about the culture you came from. But you were our baby. And then our little girl.

"You may look a certain way," she continued. "Dark hair. Dark eyes. But everyone looks different from everyone else. Really, you are just Cammy. Our little American girl."

"Well, I am an American girl," Cammy said. "But it's kind of interesting to find out what I might be eating if I were still in Vietnam."

"All you do," her mom said, "is cook the rice in coconut milk. We'll have to get some coconut milk in town. What else do you want to try?"

"I don't know anything else," Cammy said. "I'm an American girl. Remember?"

"There's a Vietnamese cafe in town," Grandma offered. "I've always wanted to eat there."

"We need to find a Vietnamese cookbook," Mom added. "Let's all ride into town while Dad and Grandpa go fishing. We'll have lunch at the Vietnamese cafe."

At the cafe, they had a big meal. First they had **spring rolls**. They dipped them in a spicy sauce. Next, they had **pho soup** and hot and sour soup.

"This soup has a good name. It is hot—and sour too!" Cammy said.

For the main course, they shared huge plates of food. They had **lo mein** with rice noodles, fried rice with shrimp and crab, and lemongrass chicken. They poured more spicy sauce over the lo mein and lemongrass chicken.

"This is good food," Cammy said.

Jill, Janelle, and Jamie mostly ate rice.

"Try some lo mein," Mom suggested.

"Yuck," Jill said. "Looks like worms."

Cammy used chopsticks.

"I wonder why all the food is in such small pieces," Cammy said. "It seems more like fork or even spoon food." It took her a long time to get the food to her mouth. But she ate the whole meal with chopsticks.

After lunch, Cammy's sisters played in the park. Her mom sat on a bench and watched them. Cammy and her grandma crossed the street to the library.

They walked up to the reference desk.

"Can you help us find out about Vietnam?" Grandma asked.

"What do you want to know? History? Customs? Geography? Travel?" the lady asked.

"Customs," Cammy piped up.

"And food," Grandma added.

"Cookbooks are on the second floor," the lady said. "Follow me. I'll show you where the other information is."

Fifteen minutes later, Cammy and Grandma were back in the park.

"We got a cookbook and two books about Vietnamese culture and customs," Cammy said.

Grandma sat down on the bench next to Cammy's mom. She opened the cookbook. "We could make the . . ." She looked up.

Cammy had run off to play with her little sisters.

"I guess I get to decide what we'll make," Grandma laughed.

7

Nuoc Mam

"Yuck!" Cammy said. She was reading the cookbook.

"This sounds awful!" she yelled. "Listen," she told her little sisters.

"You take a barrel. Then you put a lot of little fish in it."

"Like goldfish?" Jill asked.

"I guess so," Cammy said. "They're called **anchovies**. I think the fish must be dead when you do this.

"So you take the fish," she continued. "You lay them in the bottom of a barrel. You pour salt over them. Then you put more fish in. And more salt. Then more fish. And so on. You can add things like garlic, lemon, sugar, and hot peppers.

"Then you close the barrel," Cammy said. "You let it sit for three months. Or longer. Then you drain this stuff from the barrel. It's called **nuoc mam**. You eat it!"

Cammy held her nose.

Jill and Janelle held their noses too.

"It must really stink by then," Cammy said.

Her mom sat down across the table. "I think the salt does things to the fish. Remember how Grandpa likes sardines. And pickled herring? It's kind of the same thing."

"Well, I'm never eating any," Cammy said. She wrinkled her nose. She folded her arms across her chest.

"I'll eat sticky rice and fruit. And lemongrass chicken. But I'm never, ever eating nuoc mam."

Her mom smiled. "Remember that pretty little jar in the cafe?"

"The one with the little flowers on it? The one we poured on the food?" Cammy asked.

Her mom nodded.

"The one that tasted spicy?"

Her mom nodded again.

"Do you think that was nuoc mam?" Cammy asked.

"Well, it *was* called fish sauce."

"Yuck!" Cammy yelled. Then she thought for a minute. "Hmmm. Guess it didn't kill me. In fact, it was pretty good." Cammy smiled. "But let's not make any, okay?"

"Fine with me," Mom said. "We'll buy it."

8

Jamie's Thoi Noi

"No way am I giving up my birthday!" Cammy said. She had just read that the Vietnamese do not celebrate birthdays. "I'm not giving up my presents. Or my cake."

Mom smiled. "Greedy girl," she laughed. "Don't worry. You don't have to give up your birthday parties."

"Well," Cammy said. Then she changed the subject. "They do have something that's like a party. It's called **Thoi Noi**. The book says that's when a baby's first birthday is celebrated. We could do this for Jamie. She's only 14 months. So she's still close to being 1."

"How do we celebrate?" her mom asked.

Cammy showed her the book. Mom laughed.

"We'll do it tonight," Mom said. "But I'm not making another cake. What a mess!"

Mom shook her head. She was remembering. They had put the cake on the tray of Jamie's high chair.

Jamie smashed her hand into the cake. She grabbed some of it. She smeared it across her face. At last, she got some into her mouth. Then she put both hands in the cake. Before long, her face was in the cake. After that, nobody wanted any cake.

All afternoon, Cammy gathered objects. She'd choose one. Then she would put it back. She didn't want too many objects. She placed them in a circle on the floor. After dinner, the family sat around the circle of objects.

Cammy explained what each object stood for. "If Jamie chooses the compass, she'll be an explorer. The computer mouse pad means she'll work with computers. She'll be a teacher if she selects the book. If she picks the bandage, she'll be a doctor or nurse. The jar of dirt means she'll be a farmer or gardener. If she chooses the toy rocket, she'll be an astronaut. The spoon means she'll be a cook."

Dad set Jamie in the middle of the circle. She just sat there. Everyone was very quiet. No one moved.

Jamie looked at all the objects in front of her. She turned around. She began to move. She seemed to be heading for the bandage.

Then the family cat did what all

cats do. She walked where no one wanted her. Right into the circle.

Jamie grabbed Kitty's tail. Everyone laughed.

"I guess she'll be a vet," Cammy said.

9

Potluck

Cammy and her mom found a listing in the phone book. It said Vietnamese Cultural Center. Maybe they could learn more about Vietnamese ways there.

Cammy's mother called the number. She spoke with the people at the center. Before she hung up, the family had been invited to a **potluck** dinner.

Cammy met a girl just her age at the potluck. Her name was Melanie.

"My name in Vietnam was **Men**. It means 'adorable,' " Melanie explained. "I chose a name close to it. You can call me Mel, though."

Melanie had come to the U.S. about five years ago with her family. She had two smaller brothers. Mel and Cammy found that they had many things in common. They both liked to make crafts. They both liked to swim and fish. And they loved to talk on the phone.

At the potluck, Cammy tried more new foods. She tried nuoc mam again too.

"It's really good," Cammy said. "But I liked it better before I knew how it was made."

Cammy tried fruits she had never heard of. There was *xoai*, or mango. Cammy ate a different kind of banana. The **pomelo** tasted like grapefruit. And the **chom chom** was a sweet treat.

"I'll show you the Vietnamese way to play tug-of-war," Mel said. She grabbed a boy. He was 12 too. His name was **Liem**.

"We don't use a rope," Melanie explained. Liem grabbed both of Cammy's hands. He had a big smile on his face. Melanie got behind Cammy. She put her arms around Cammy's waist. She wove her fingers together in front.

"Now all you kids get behind us," Mel said. "Hold on to the waist of the person in front of you."

The boys got behind Liem. The girls got behind Cammy.

Melanie yelled, "Okay, when I count to three, pull! The side that pulls apart first loses.

"Ready? One. Two. Three. Pull!"

Liem had strong hands. Cammy couldn't let go if she wanted to. Everyone was laughing and pulling. The line went back and forth. But it seemed to be moving in Liem's direction.

Cammy's line started to sway sideways. The last part of the line fell on the floor laughing. They jumped up.

"Let's do it again!" they all sang. "We can beat the boys!"

They played games until the storyteller appeared. Then everyone got quiet. They gathered in a circle around her.

10

One Hundred Children

They sat on the floor in front of the storyteller. She bowed her head. She became very still. Then she looked up and began to speak. Her hands danced in front of her as she told this story.

One Hundred Children

This is the story of how we Vietnamese came to be.

Long, long ago there lived a mighty king. This king had a special magic. He could change shapes. He could be a dragon or a snake. He could be a tiger or a monster. Most of the time he was a dragon. He lived in the Underwater World. His name was Dragon King.

One day, Dragon King followed a stream from the Underwater World. It took him far north into the mountains. There, he found the goddess **Au Co**.

Au Co had magic also. She had great beauty too. Her skin was as white as a grain of rice. Her mouth was like the new **lotus** blossom. Her hair was as shiny and black as the sea at night.

The Dragon King saw her from afar. He fell in love.

Au Co sat on a stone. She looked over the mountains ahead. She saw something coming toward her. It seemed to be a huge elephant. Yes, it was.

The elephant came to Au Co. It picked her up with its trunk and put her on its back. Then it carried her away. The elephant carried Au Co over the mountains. At last, they came to a beautiful valley. The elephant put Au Co down.

Before her eyes, the elephant became a dragon. He had shiny scales of many colors. His flashing green eyes looked into hers.

"Will you be my bride?" asked the Dragon King.

Au Co fell in love at once. She began to cry with joy. Her tears formed the trees and grasses. They made the flowers and all living things.

"I will marry you," said Au Co.

So Au Co and the Dragon King settled into the valley. They spent many years together. Some were good. Some were bad. You see, they were opposites. Like the **yin and yang.** Like fire and water.

One day, Au Co gave birth. But remember, this birth came from the union of a dragon and a goddess. Au Co did not give birth to a baby. Instead, it was a bag of one hundred eggs.

The Dragon King took the bag to a field. There it lay in the warm sunshine. After seven days, the eggs hatched.

Out of each egg came a child. One hundred perfect children. Each child was beautiful, smart, and full of courage. Each child had a lovely name. Star, Moon, Flower, Water, Leaf, Air, Sun, and Light were some of the names.

Au Co and Dragon King cared deeply for their children. They taught them to plant and harvest rice. They taught them to love and honor one another.

Often, though, Dragon King went back to his Underwater World. Then Au Co and the children were left alone.

Once, it rained for many months. A terrible flood came. The children called out, "Father, why aren't you here to save us from the flood?"

Soon, a large fish appeared. He swam through the flood. He drank the water as he swam back to the Underwater World. He spit the water where it belonged.

The fish turned back into the Dragon King. Once again, he stayed in the Underwater World. Au Co and the children were again left alone.

Au Co called out, "Where are you? Why do you leave us alone? We need you."

The Dragon King appeared. Au Co said, "I came from the North. I bore you one hundred perfect children. Now you leave me and the children alone. I have become like a widow."

The Dragon King answered, "I am of the dragon breed. The king of the water breeds. I must live in the Underwater World. You are a goddess. You must live in the highlands. In the North."

"We are too different. We don't belong together," the Dragon King said. "We are like the yin and the yang. Like fire and water. We must go our own ways.

"I will take 50 children with me," he added. "We will go to the Underwater World. You take 50 children to the North.

"Though we go to the mountains or the sea, we will remember each other. If anything happens, we will let the other know."

So the Dragon King and Au Co went their separate ways. He to the Underwater World. She to the mountains. He to the South. She to the North.

Their children were free to be with their father or mother. They could go underwater. Or they could

50

go to the mountains. And so it has been for many thousands of years.

The end

The storyteller told more stories. She told about the genies of the hearth. And she told a tale that was very much like a Cinderella story.

It was late when Cammy and her family left the potluck.

"I'll call you!" Melanie yelled.

Cammy waved. She was tired. But she was very happy. She had met other people from Vietnam. She had made a friend. And she had been given two jobs.

11

Cammy's Jobs

At the potluck, Cammy learned that
people in Vietnam needed help. The wars
had torn the country apart. Some villages
had no water. Land that had once been
used for planting was ruined. Many
people were sick and hurt. Many
children still roamed the streets. The
new government had problems too.

This made Cammy very sad. She had been lucky. Her parents had saved her. Probably saved her life. Now, she wanted to help.

A woman at the potluck said to learn more. She told Cammy to read as much as she could about Vietnam. She advised Cammy to read newspapers, magazines, and books. The woman said that when Cammy knew more, then she could help her people.

So Cammy made a plan. She would spend Sunday afternoons at the library—as many Sundays as it took.

Her goal was to read all she could about Vietnam. She wanted to learn its history, culture, politics, economy, and problems.

When she was done, she would know how she could help the people of Vietnam.

Cammy's second job had to be done by the time **Tet** came around. Cammy had heard about Tet. But her family had never celebrated it.

Tet is the Vietnamese New Year. It is a month or two after the U.S. New Year. School was just starting. So Cammy had about six months to do her job. Melanie was working on it too.

Melanie and Cammy's job was to make yellow paper flowers. They were to put sparkly red sequins in the centers. Cammy tied the flowers on to willow branches. They looked like **mai** blossoms. These blossoms bloom in Vietnam during Tet.

So, for the next six months, Cammy and Melanie made mai blossoms. They made six big boxes full!

Just before Tet, Cammy and Mel took the mai blossoms to the meeting hall. They hung the blossoms everywhere. Others had made decorations too. The hall looked very pretty.

Then Cammy helped her mom and dad clean the house. Her sisters helped too. They cleaned from top to bottom.

"During Tet, the house cannot be cleaned," Cammy explained. "You might sweep out the genies of the hearth. Or the genies of good fortune. Besides, you want to start the New Year clean," she added.

Soon, the house was shining. Mom looked around her nice neat house. "This Tet is a great thing," she said.

Cammy and her sisters got new clothes.

"Do you and Daddy have any **debts**?" Cammy asked her mom.

"Well, yes," her mom said. "Why?"

"It's best to celebrate Tet debt-free," Cammy advised.

"Well," Mom said. "If we could pay off the house and the car, we would. We'll just have to celebrate Tet in debt." She laughed.

"Anything else?" Mom asked.

"Do you and Dad have new clothes?" Cammy asked.

"I do have that new sweater," Mom said. "I'll wear it. And I just got Dad some new socks. You can tell him to put them on."

When Tet came, Cammy's family was ready. The house was clean. They had made food. And the night of the Tet celebration, everyone in Cammy's family wore something new.

12

Tet

The hall looked beautiful. Tiny lights had been strung across the ceiling. They twinkled like stars. The mai-blossom decorations sparkled along the walls.

Everyone was dressed up. Many girls and women wore pretty **ao dais**. An ao dai is a long, formfitting dress. It has sleeves and a high collar.

People gave one another red envelopes. The envelopes had "good luck" money in them. Melanie ran across the hall. She had a red envelope in her hand.

"For you," she told Cammy.

Cammy reached into her pocket. "And for you," she smiled. She handed Mel a red envelope too.

Music was playing. "This is **nhac vang**," Melanie told Cammy. "It's golden music. It's about love. And it's about being your own person. It's made here now. It can't be played in Vietnam."

"How sad," Cammy said. Then she gave her friend a hug. "Well, I'm glad you're over here with me now. Let's celebrate that."

People were dancing. The boy who had played tug-of-war months earlier spotted Cammy. He stared for a while. Then he walked over.

"He's heading this way!" Melanie said.

"Yikes," said Cammy. That's all she got out before Liem asked her to dance.

"I don't really know how to dance," she said.

"Me neither," Liem said. "We'll just pretend that we do."

He led her to the dance floor. Liem put his left hand on the back of Cammy's waist. Then he took her left hand in his right hand. Cammy didn't know what to do with her right hand. Finally, she laid it on his shoulder. They began to step in time to the music. They shuffled back and forth.

Suddenly, Liem stopped.

"I'm sorry," he said. "This is backwards."

Cammy looked puzzled. Liem let go of Cammy's hand. He then put his right hand on the back of her waist. He held her right hand in his left. Cammy put her left hand on Liem's shoulder.

"Does this feel better?" he asked.

"Both ways feel kind of strange," Cammy said.

Finally, the song was over. Everyone clapped.

"Maybe we can dance again," Liem said.

"Maybe they'll play a fast song for us," Cammy smiled.

Liem didn't ask Cammy to dance again. But he watched her from across the room for the rest of the night.

"He likes you," Mel teased.

"I kind of like him too," Cammy smiled.

The party lasted late into the night. There was lots of food. Cammy's favorite food was Earth cakes and Sky cakes. Some people sang. Others put on special costumes and did dances.

At the end of the party, everyone went outside. They gathered around a heap of firecrackers in the parking lot.

"The noise will scare away evil spirits left from last year," Cammy explained to her family. "We will all start the New Year in peace."

"Stand back!" a man yelled. He made everyone move to the edges of the lot. Then he lit the firecrackers.

A thousand *POPs* went off.

Everyone cheered.

Last year was very special for me, Cammy thought. But next year will be even better.

Epilogue

❦

Pleiku, Vietnam—2000

A 12-year-old girl stood in line with her family. She looked a lot like Cammy had at that age. Her long, black hair fell loosely down her back. At last, it was her turn.

The doctor checked the girl's heart and blood pressure. She felt the glands in the girl's neck. She smiled at the girl.

"You remind me of myself at your age," she said in Vietnamese. A shy grin came across the girl's face. She ducked her head.

"Do you go to school?" the doctor asked. The girl nodded. They smiled at each other.

"Do you hurt anywhere?" the doctor asked.

"No," the girl said.

The doctor handed the girl a small medicine cup.

"Drink this in one gulp," the doctor said. "Okay. All done."

The girl moved on. Her empty cup was in her hand.

The doctor turned to her next patient.

The doctor wasn't really a doctor. Not yet, anyway. She was in training. She still had a few more years of medical school.

Her school had sponsored a trip to Vietnam. The medical students had come with a group of doctors. They volunteered at a free clinic.

Cammy's dream had come true. She was in Vietnam. Not to stay. But to help. And she would come back again. To help.

After all, she owed it to her parents. All of them. Her parents in America. Her parents in Vietnam. And Au Co and the Dragon King.

Glossary

ambush

to be attacked

anchovy

small fish used as a food decoration or in sauces and relishes

ao dai (ow zi)

long formfitting dress with sleeves and a high collar

Au Co (o ka)

goddess

bobber

small floating object, usually round and plastic, that attaches to a fishing line. When a fish strikes, the bobber will go under the water, alerting the fisher that a fish has taken the bait.

chom chom

tropical sweet fruit with a red, spiny skin

Communist	person who believes that government should be centralized under one person and that all citizens are equal and property should be owned by all in common
debt	something owed
democratic	having all people rule either directly or indirectly
draft	to be ordered into military service
front	something used to hide the true activity of a person
guerrilla warfare	fighting methods, such as sneak attacks, usually used by the weaker side to avoid large battles

interpreter	person who translates orally for people who speak different languages
Liem (lem)	Vietnamese name
lo mein (low main)	Vietnamese dish made with noodles that look like spaghetti
lotus	type of water lily
mai (my)	flower
Men (men)	Vietnamese name
nhac vang (nak van)	popular music, usually romantic
nuoc mam (nook mom)	spicy sauce made from fish for Vietnamese food
orphanage	place where children without parents are taken care of

pho soup (pron fa)	Vietnamese soup made from chicken or beef broth with spices added
Pleiku (play KOO)	city in the central highlands of South Vietnam
pomelo	fruit similar to a grapefruit
potluck	meal where everyone brings food to share
pull out	to leave or withdraw
rebel	to oppose by taking up arms against a government
Saigon (SIGH gone)	former capital of South Vietnam, now called Ho Chi Minh City
spring roll	appetizer with vegetables and sometimes meat rolled in an egg roll wrapper and fried

Tet	the Vietnamese New Year observed for three days beginning on the first new moon after January 20
Thoi Noi (toy noy)	celebration held when a child turns one
Vietcong (vee et KONG)	guerrilla (see glossary entry) member of the Vietnamese Communist (see glossary entry) movement
Vietminh (vee et MIN)	person who followed the Vietnamese Communist movement from 1941 to 1951
xoai (swee)	Vietnamese word for "mango"

yin and yang   Chinese principle of a feminine and masculine being that combine in nature to produce all things